THE GHOSTLY TALES OF BURLINGTON

Published by Arcadia Children's Books
A Division of Arcadia Publishing
Charleston, SC
www.arcadiapublishing.com

First published 2022

Manufactured in the United States

ISBN 978-1-4671-9864-6

Library of Congress Control Number: 2022933028

All images courtesy of Shutterstock.com; p. 2 mkzdillon/Shutterstock.com;
p. 44 Harold Stiver/Shutterstock.com; p. 52 julie deshaies/Shutterstock.com;
p. 92 Malachi Jacobs/Shutterstock.com.

Spooky America

The Ghostly Tales of Burlington

Carie Juettner

Adapted from *Haunted Burlington* by Thea Lewis

arcadia
CHILDREN'S BOOKS

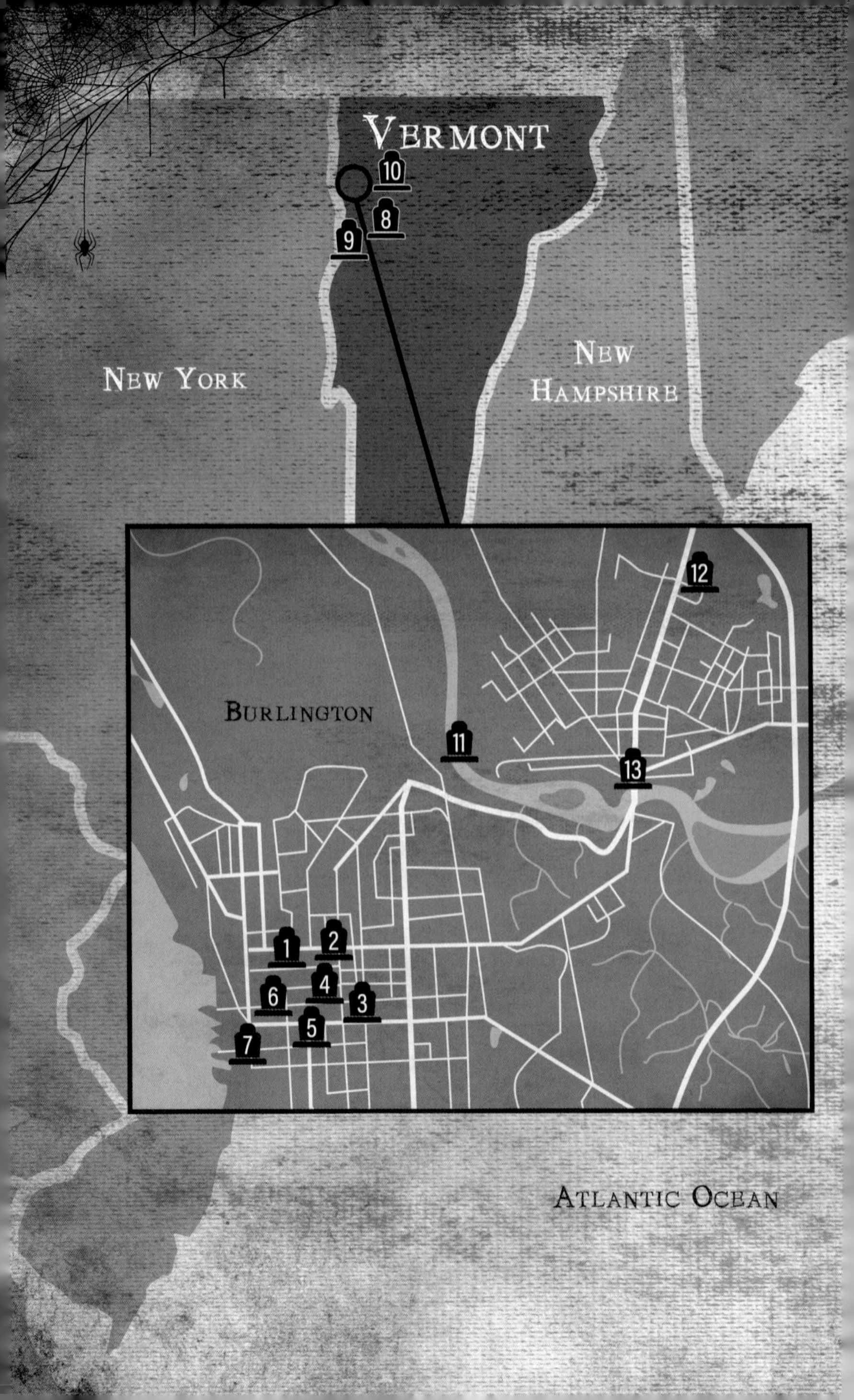

Vermont
10
8
9
New York
New Hampshire
Burlington
12
11
13
1
2
4
6
3
5
7
Atlantic Ocean

Table of Contents & Map Key

Burlington

Introduction: Who Put the "Boo" in Burlington?

Burlington, Vermont, is a scenic city located on the eastern shore of Lake Champlain. Home to interesting architecture, beautiful nature areas, great restaurants, and the University of Vermont, it's no wonder that residents and tourists alike enjoy spending time in this charming town. The Church Street Marketplace offers a unique shopping experience, and guests can enjoy a lovely view of the Adirondack Mountains from Waterfront Park. But visitors sometimes end up finding more than they bargained for.

Ghosts dwell in every nook and cranny of Burlington. So many spirits abound, in fact, that it's hard to see a show, go shopping, or walk a trail without running into one. So, the question is, who put the boo in Burlington? Where did all these restless spirits come from?

Within these pages, you'll meet the ghosts of Burlington's founders, the spirit of a brave firefighter, victims of tragic accidents, and even a man who used to attend funerals for fun. From spooky shopping malls to haunted homes, you'll hear stories of how Burlington's past is still alive in the present. There have even been mysterious happenings at a McDonald's!

While a few of the stories may leave you with a comforting feeling, some of the tales are quite terrifying, so turn on the lights and make sure no one *uninvited* is reading over your shoulder. Then get comfy and enjoy getting to know Burlington's ghosts.

CHAPTER 1

The Haunted Mall

What do you think of when you picture a shopping mall? Big department stores and trendy clothing boutiques? Food courts and movie theaters? Kiosks selling every trinket imaginable, and aisles crowded with families. How about mysterious sounds that have no source and people who vanish right before your eyes? No? Well, then maybe you never visited Burlington's mall.

Burlington Square Mall, which later changed its name to Burlington Town Center, opened in 1976 at 49 Church Street in the heart of Burlington. The shopping center had all the things you expect to find in a mall . . . and a few things you don't. Employees who worked at the Burlington Town Center agree the place was haunted.

In 1999, the mall opened a new department store called Filene's, and a young woman became the manager of the cosmetics counter. Part of her job included unpacking and displaying the merchandise, which meant staying late after the store was closed, carefully arranging perfume bottles and makeup in the glass cases.

One night, she was working alone, hurrying to finish her tasks so she could go home. She gathered an armful of empty boxes and took them to the storage room in the back, but when she opened the door, she got a shock. Standing in the corner of the room amongst boxes of merchandise was a man in a dark suit and a tall black hat. He had a beard and bushy sideburns. He simply looked at her, not saying anything.

Confused, but still wanting to take control of the situation, the manager said, "Excuse me? May I help you?" At that point, the man disappeared into thin air.

The woman was certainly unnerved by the experience. Wouldn't you be? Still, she didn't tell anyone about it for a long time. She was too afraid people might not believe her and think she was not well. She was even worried she might lose her job.

Finally, after weeks of keeping her supernatural sighting to herself, the young manager became friends with another woman, older than her, who worked in the women's clothing department. Over lunch one day, the new friend hesitantly shared a story of something strange that had happened to her in the store.

One night, she told the younger woman, just as Filene's was closing, she was organizing the receipts from her cash register and tidying up for the night when she heard a baby crying. She'd thought the store was empty. The announcement that Filene's was closing had already been made, and she hadn't seen anyone when she checked the ladies' room a few minutes before. But the baby's wailing grew louder until there was no denying it came from the restroom. Impatient to close up shop and get home, she returned to the ladies' room to tell the customer with the baby that the store had closed, and they needed to leave. The saleswoman, expecting to find a mom changing a diaper, was not prepared for what she saw.

There was no baby in the restroom. Instead, when she opened the door, she saw a woman in an old-fashioned nightgown and cap. The woman wore a deeply sad expression on her face, and her arms were stretched out in front of her as if she were trying to grasp something. Almost as soon as the saleswoman saw her, she disappeared. The crying stopped. No baby was discovered in the store.

"I couldn't help but think," she said, nervously finishing her tale, "that the sad woman in the restroom had also been searching for that crying baby."

Mixed with the shivers that her new friend's story sent through her, the manager of the cosmetics department also felt a flood of relief. She wasn't the only person who had seen a ghost at Filene's! She immediately told her friend about her own otherworldly encounter.

Empowered by each other's experiences, the friends began asking around to find out if they were the only ones who had witnessed something paranormal. They weren't. The security guard at Filene's had also seen strange sights . . . on video!

The store had recently installed a new security system, excellent by the day's standards. The first time the security guard and his boss watched one of the recorded tapes, they saw something odd. Blurry shapes and circular lights drifted to and fro across the screen. These smudges could be seen even in recordings that included no customers or staff, just empty escalators, and vacant aisles. The security team believed they had a faulty tape, but when they ran the system the following night with a new tape, the same thing happened.

Filene's wasn't the only store in Burlington Town Center with unexplained occurrences. Strange things were also going on at The Limited. Employees at the trendy clothing store had trouble keeping up with their belongings. They would place their bags and coats somewhere at the start of their shift, but when it was time to leave, the stuff was gone. The things always turned up eventually. Nothing was ever stolen, so no real harm was done, but everyone agreed that an unseen hand was moving the items.

Purses and jackets weren't the only thing the sneaky spirit liked to play with. One night after closing, the manager and one employee stayed late to steam the wrinkles out of the outfits on display. When the manager went to the storage room to put the steamer away, she heard a rattling sound behind her. Aware that she was alone in the room, the woman froze in place as the rattling became louder and louder. When she finally found the courage to turn around, her eyes landed on the rack of empty hangers in the corner. Every single hanger was shaking violently! In an instant, the manager was shaking too. She ran back out to the sales floor and told her employee it was time for them to get out of there.

Who would choose to haunt a mall? And why were the ghosts that revealed themselves in Filene's dressed in nineteenth century clothing? Some believe that experiences can leave a "psychic imprint" on a place, meaning that a person's energy can live on even after they are gone. Maybe the people who inhabited the land beneath the haunted mall left powerful impressions in their wake.

The Burlington Town Center closed in 2017 and became CityPlace Burlington. As of the writing of this book, the location is under construction. But just because the structure is gone doesn't mean the ghosts are too. You can remodel the buildings but determined spirits will always find a home to haunt, so whoever ends up at 49 Church Street in Burlington should be on the lookout for some company.

F
O
D

CHAPTER 2

Would You Like Fries with Your Ghost?

Burlington is known for its many haunted restaurants. Nectar's on Main Street has been serving up good food, live music, and spooky spirits for more than forty years. Employees there have reported a grumpy ghost in the kitchen as well as the phantoms of two small children who visit the place. And customers at the American Flatbread Company on St. Paul should steer clear of the basement where the ghost of a former employee seems to think it's funny to trap people inside the walk-in freezer. But perhaps the most unusual, haunted eatery in Burlington was the McDonald's.

Yep, McDonald's. The fast-food place had all the regular menu items—Big Macs, fries, milkshakes, and Happy Meals—but this particular Golden Arches also served a side of spookiness.

The possessed McDonald's is no longer open. The site at 160 Bank Street is now the home of the Farm House Tap & Grill. But back in the 80's when the location was the site of the famous burger chain, all sorts of strange things used to happen there. For instance, things used to move around during the night. The manager's binder of closing instructions frequently went missing between the time she locked up and the time she arrived again the next day. It always turned up in odd places.

The manager also kept a sweater at work for cold days when the constantly opening doors let in the chilly Vermont winds. One day, the sweater disappeared. The employees looked everywhere for it, but unlike the binder, the sweater didn't turn up. Several days later, when the manager arrived for her shift, a coworker handed her the sweater. When she asked him where he found it, he said it had been folded neatly and sitting on a sink in the men's restroom. She certainly hadn't left it there!

Eerie sounds also plagued the McDonald's. Employees on the late shift sometimes heard people talking while they were cleaning up after the restaurant had closed. The youthful voices either whispered to each other or called out across the open space, but no person was ever found. A man who worked the early shift heard disembodied voices too. He said it sounded like children laughing.

Other sounds also invaded the atmosphere of sizzling burgers and soda machines and cash registers. People reported noises that sounded like a ball bouncing and an accordion playing and something heavy sliding back and forth, but the sources of these sounds were never discovered.

Why would a ghost choose to haunt a McDonald's? The answer may originate from the building that existed there before. 160 Bank Street was once the home of the Black Cat Café, a restaurant and music club that dated back to the 1930s. Up until the 1970s, the Black Cat was still a popular hangout in Burlington, until tragedy struck. In 1977, a gas explosion destroyed the building, taking the lives of the owner and his two sons.

Such a heartbreaking disaster would leave a mark on a place. Even though the building was demolished, and a new structure built for the McDonald's, it's no wonder that some psychic energy remained from the devastation of the Black Cat Café.

CHAPTER 3

Phantoms of the Opera House

Most people have heard of the Phantom of the Opera, but the phantoms of the Howard Opera House in Burlington have stuck around long after the music stopped.

John Purple Howard was a rich man who used his wealth to benefit Burlington in the late 1800s. He paid to restore buildings at the university, donated statues, and other decorative enhancements to various locations, and even helped to improve the city's cemeteries. So, when Howard built his opera house on Church Street in 1888, he spared no expense to make it one of a kind. Howard hired Steven D. Hatch, an architect who had designed beautiful hotels in New York. Together, they created one of Burlington's most distinguished buildings.

Although operas were performed at the Howard Opera House, the building provided much more than its name implies. The theater was housed on the upper level, leaving the first floor open for shops, and the space hosted plays, holiday celebrations, and graduation ceremonies in addition to operas.

John Howard built the opera house, but Belle Walker came to think of it as hers.

Belle's father-in-law, Kilburn Walker, managed the theater, and when he passed away, she took over. Belle was a sharp businesswoman whose combination of charm and smart business decisions earned her the reputation of one of the best theatrical managers in the country.

Despite the theater's popularity and Belle's excellent job running it, the Howard Opera House was soon forced to close its doors. According to insurance companies, the location of the theater space on the second floor was dangerous, and their rates were too high to pay. On November 30, 1904, after the house's last performance of a play called *Our Pastor*, Belle Walker came out on stage and received applause from the audience while the orchestra played "Auld Lang Syne." It was a bittersweet end to her career with her beloved theater.

Although performances at the Opera House ceased over a century ago, the magnificent structure still stands on Church Street, and it has served many purposes over the years. Some of the employees and business owners who have worked in the building say it has a few phantoms.

For a time, the Howard Opera House was home to clothing stores such as Magrams and April Cornell. The Magrams department store was a fixture in Burlington for decades, as was the Otis elevator inside. This old-fashioned elevator was the kind with a bronze gate and manual controls. Instead of pushing a button and waiting for the elevator to do its job, an attendee inside would ask you where you wanted to go, then pull the levers to operate the elevator and take to you to your floor.

A man named Robert Krupp operated the Magrams elevator for twenty years. He was well-known in Burlington and loved by all. His charm and friendly conversation created a cheerful atmosphere at Magrams. The department store closed in the 1990s, and Mr. Krupp passed away in 2001, but some say he's still hanging around the old building. People have described a "helpful" spirit that reminds them of the old elevator operator.

If only all ghosts could be as helpful and compassionate as Robert Krupp. Meredith O'Neil and her friend Sharon say whoever haunted the April Cornell clothing store wasn't as friendly. When they worked there, the back room always made people feel uneasy, and strange things happened there. Objects would fly off the shelves for no reason, and employees would hear footsteps even when no one else was in the store. The CD player in the back room would often stop halfway through the first song, and when they went to check it, the power button would be off, as if someone had purposely turned off the music. Meredith even saw an actual ghost one night. When she went to close, there was a man in a dark suit and a fedora hat sitting on a bench in the back room. Meredith didn't stay long enough to ask who he was, she just ran!

From 1985 to 1998, an independent bookstore called Chassman & Bem made its home in one section of the opera house building, and someone or some*thing* used to cause the booksellers there lots of trouble. One of their favorite targets was the children's books section.

Employees working in the Chassman & Bem's kid section would sometimes turn their backs on a six-foot-tall wooden bookcase for no more than a moment, only to turn back around and see that an entire shelf of the previously organized bookcase was empty.

Where were the children's books that had been on the shelf a moment before? They were on the carpet. Now, you may be thinking, *Hold on, wait a second. Maybe the books just fell off the shelf. Or maybe someone pushed them out from the other side.* But there was no way the books could have been pushed. It was impossible to get behind the bookcase because it was bolted to the wall. And if the books had simply fallen, then why were they laying on the floor in alphabetical order by the author's last name?

The unseen prankster created havoc so frequently that the clerks at Chassman & Bem didn't like to be the one closing up at night.

They started to worry they might accidentally take someone (or some*thing*) home with them when they left.

The uncanny phenomena at Chassman & Bem wasn't entirely confined to the children's section. A young woman who worked at the basement office of the bookstore who was sensitive to psychic energy felt a constant presence when she was at work. For her, the sensations in the Opera House were not positive. She was very unhappy while working there.

The Howard Opera House has such a long and unique history, it's hard to know who all of these phantoms might be, but it's safe to bet that if spirits are haunting the building, Belle Walker, the former manager, is probably among them. It's understandable that a woman who took such great care of the Opera House would want to keep an eye on it. Who knows? She could be the ghost turning off the CD player. Maybe the employees need to play a little opera music once in a while for Belle.

CHAPTER 4

Heroism Never Dies

Firefighters are heroes. As first responders, these men and women must possess the courage and calm, the strength and swiftness to douse a burning building or run headlong into danger to save another human being. We remain grateful to them for their service and are in awe of their bravery and compassion.

Back in the 1800s in Vermont, firefighting wasn't just a job, it was also a sport. Fire teams traveled long distances to compete in a contest called a Fireman's Muster. Fire departments were made up of volunteers, and back then they consisted entirely of men.

In September of 1878, a fire team from Burlington made history at the annual Fireman's Muster in Chicago. The Barnes Hose Company went up against twenty-two teams from around the country in an event that required them to pull a hose cart weighing five hundred pounds for three hundred yards. (That's like pulling a full-grown grizzly bear across three football fields!) When they reached their destination, the team had to unroll three hundred feet of heavy hose, attach it to a hydrant, and produce a stream of water. The Barnes team from Burlington won the competition by completing the difficult task in sixty-two and a half seconds, just over one minute! They set a record with their time that was never broken.

Although the Fireman's Muster was a great way for fire teams to show off their skills and stay fit for the job, rivalries can also be a bad thing. Within the city of Burlington, teams competed to be the first at a fire, and this sometimes caused conflict. Legend has it that two teams once showed up at the same time and argued so long about who got there first that the building they came to save burned down. To add even more ridiculousness to the tale, that building was a fire station.

These days, the men and women who fight fires have the aid of modern equipment and technology that helps them do their very dangerous jobs. But back in the 1800s, when fire engines were still drawn by horses, firefighters didn't have that extra support. And no matter what technology you do or don't have, fires can be very unpredictable, especially in the cold Vermont climate.

In January of 1885, a fire broke out in the Holt Spool and Bobbin Factory just south of downtown Burlington. The sawdust and wood shavings from the manufacture of the wooden spools combined with the cold, dry winter air to make the fire spread quickly. While the workers fled, Mr. Holt, the owner of the factory, did what he could to try to contain the blaze, but it was too fast for him. The flames quickly created an inferno that reached the boiler room, and Mr. Holt had to flee as well.

Luckily, help was on the way from the Ethan Allan Engine Company. The Ethans, as the firefighters from that station were called, hurried to Holt's factory to combat the raging blaze. Among them was a man named Edwin C. Parker. Edwin was thirty-four years old, and was originally from Westford, but he had lived in Burlington for about eight years and was well-respected in town. Edwin was an honest, polite, thoughtful gentleman. His regular job was clerk for a clothing store, but Edwin's passion was fighting fires. As a volunteer at the fire station, Edwin had earned a reputation for his courage and determination under pressure. He was calm and reliable in the most dangerous situations, and his skill at firefighting had recently earned him a promotion to fire assistant.

Edwin and the other Ethans were the first to arrive at the scene of the burning factory, followed shortly by the Boxers, another fire team. But the building was already engulfed, and the strong winds fanned the flames. To make matters worse, the hydrants on Champlain Street were frozen, so the firefighters had to connect their hoses on Pine Street instead and stretch them through an alley to the burning factory.

Unable to save the building, the fire crews focused their attention on the dry house attached to the main structure, in hopes of saving the merchandise inside. When the nozzle on the Ethans' hose became clogged by a stone, Edwin immediately ran toward their cart for a new one. However, right at that moment, the factory's engine room exploded, sending an enormous pile of rubble down on the brave firefighter. Edwin was killed instantly.

The town mourned the loss of their beloved fire assistant. His coffin was draped with the banner of the fire station that he loved so much.

But even death could not keep Edwin Parker from the job that he loved. After his passing, the other firefighters began to experience strange things at the Ethan Allen Engine Company. They felt like they were being watched by someone they couldn't see and sometimes heard someone moving around in the equipment room when no one was there. Ghostly footsteps followed them through the halls, keeping pace with them as they did their work. The crew even felt Edwin's presence in the new station that was built after the fire assistant's death. Noises in the tower where

they hung hoses to dry suggested that an unseen hand was rearranging the hoses, even when the tower was empty.

Today, the old Ethan Allen Engine Company on Church Street is the home of the Firehouse Center for the Visual Arts, but some say it's still haunted. A woman working there stayed late one night to finish up some tasks. When the custodian left for the evening, he stopped by her office to let her know she was the last person in the building. So, she was confused a little while later when she heard the elevator start up. Curious, the woman sat at her desk in her basement office and waited. Through her open door, she had a clear view of the elevator, which is in the place where the building's old hose-drying tower used to be. Sure enough, the light above the elevator lit up, and its doors opened wide. No one was there. They remained open for a few moments, as if waiting for a passenger to depart, before closing again. The woman decided it was time to go home for the night.

If Edwin Parker is haunting his old job, he's not alone. It turns out that most of the fire stations in Burlington have stories about ghosts. In the early 1900s, when Fire Station #3 on Mansfield Avenue was still using horse-drawn carriages to fight fires, the men on duty woke to the sound of the horses in distress. When they hurried downstairs to find out what was bothering them, they found the entire team harnessed and ready to go. That's when they realized a building across the street was on fire.

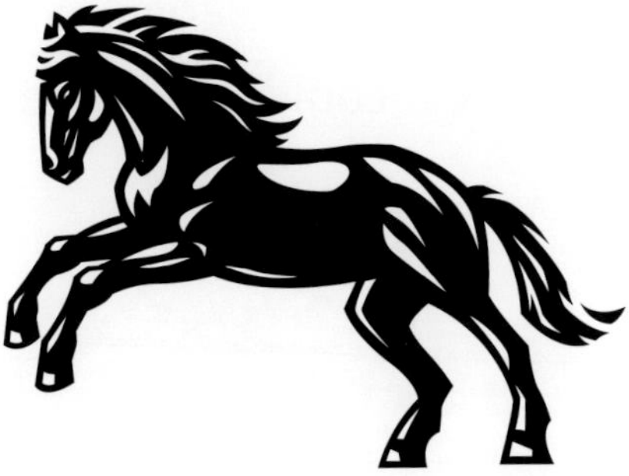

The spirit that harnessed the horses was obviously trying to be helpful, but what about the one upstairs in the barracks? Firefighters at Station #3 say if you sleep in the bed by the window, around three o'clock in the morning, you'll wake to the sensation of someone getting into bed with you! I guess someone isn't happy with the new guys taking their bunk.

Stations #1 and #5 have also been the site of some spooky situations. The crew at #1 says that their deceased fire chief still rings the alarm bell sometimes, and a firefighter at #5 was so scared, he hung a crucifix in his room for protection.

Some believe these ghosts are spirits of firefighters who stuck around the place they loved and served after death. Others think they could be victims of fires. Burlington's brave first responders always do their best to save everyone, but occasionally a person

doesn't make it. Some firefighters think the spirits of those who perished in a fire just get on the truck and come back to the firehouse with them.

It makes sense in a way. Who wouldn't want to spend some time with the heroic firefighters of Burlington?

The Flynn Theater

CHAPTER 5

The Flynn Ghost

Some ghosts aren't satisfied with abandoned buildings and drafty basements. They crave a little more *drama*. Whether you're a performer nervously waiting backstage for your big moment in the spotlight or an audience member excitedly anticipating the curtain's rise, it's easy to get caught up in the thrill of a theater. Maybe that's why so many people choose to hang around in them after they die.

Playhouses all over the United States share their stages with spirits, and Burlington's Flynn Theater is no exception.

John J. Flynn built his theater in 1930, and it immediately became a landmark on Burlington's Main Street. The theater's huge stage provided an excellent view from any seat, and visitors were captivated by its décor. For over ninety years, the Flynn Theater has offered entertainment ranging from vaudeville performances and movies to Broadway shows. And in the wings? The Flynn Ghost.

The ghost of Burlington's theater doesn't want to be the star of the show. He tends to hang out behind the scenes instead. He's been seen dozens of times by technicians and crew members of the Lyric Theater Company, a group of volunteers who helped the restore the Flynn Theater in the 80s and continues to perform there. They say the ghost is most often present when someone is working up high or doing something dangerous.

Imagine this: It's two o'clock in the morning, and you and a friend are the last two volunteers left at the theater. You're exhausted from a long day, but you're still up, working fifty feet above the stage rigging up scenery for an upcoming show. You hear someone say your name, so you turn to your friend and ask, "What?" He says he didn't say anything. It happens again, but your friend still swears he didn't speak. This time, when you turn back around, you see a man wearing gray coveralls sitting casually on a narrow rail, his legs dangling carelessly over the empty stage far below. Frozen in confusion, you stare at the man without speaking. He gives you a salute, then disappears.

I don't know what you would do if you saw a man vanish right before your eyes, but the two men from the Lyric Theater Company who saw the Flynn Ghost one night promptly decided they were finished working and went home. Now, whether they were able to sleep after that experience is unknown.

No one knows who the Flynn Ghost is, but he's always dressed the same way, in gray coveralls, dusty black boots, and a smile. His outfit looks like the kind that might have been worn by a construction worker in the 1930s. Because of this, some people wonder if the ghost is the spirit of someone who died while building the theater. Perhaps he fell to his death while performing a dangerous task high

up in the rafters of the building, and now he appears to watch over those in similar peril.

Although it's not clear if there's any truth behind this story, the ghost does seem to be a protective spirit. One woman became tangled in electrical cords while working near the catwalk, the narrow bridge extending over the stage. She lost her footing and was just about to fall when she spotted the Flynn Ghost and was suddenly able to regain her balance.

In fact, the catwalk is one of the ghost's favorite places to haunt. Just ask Meredith Neary, another member of the Lyric Theater Company. She was working behind the scenes for a performance of *The Secret Garden*. Between her duties, she would sit on the catwalk and watch the show from above. During one of these breaks, she looked over and realized she wasn't alone. About fifteen feet away, the Flynn Ghost sat perched on a crossbeam. Meredith knew immediately who he was because the spot where he was sitting wasn't reachable for non-ghosts. The heating and air conditioning units blocked the path for the living. But there he sat, comfortably swinging his legs, keeping an eye on her.

Whoever the Flynn Ghost is, his heart seems to be in the right place. Whether he's a protective spirit watching over the crew or just someone who loves the stage, he's obviously not doing any harm. Next time you visit the Flynn Theater, remember to thank all the hardworking people behind the scenes, both those you can see and those you can't.

The Follett House

CHAPTER 6

Legends of the Follett House

No ghost tour in Burlington would be complete without a stop at the Follett House. Visitors to this historic site often claim to see shadows drifting past the windows or shapes that seem to peer out at the grounds below, even when the building is closed. This just proves how active the spirits who haunt the place still are, which is no surprise considering the people who originally lived there led such interesting lives.

Timothy Follett was born in Bennington, Vermont, on January 5, 1793. Timothy was a young boy when his father died, and he and his mother and sister moved to Burlington. The move opened opportunities for young Timothy. By age thirteen, he was already impressing people with his intelligence and work ethic. Timothy graduated from the University of Vermont and worked for a legislator for a few years before moving in with his sister Fanny and her husband, Eleazer H. Deming. Deming, a successful businessman, paid for Timothy to attend law school.

Headstrong and ambitious, Follett graduated from law school and held positions as a lawyer, state's attorney, and county court judge all before he was thirty years old. At that time, his health began to bother

him. Needing a less stressful schedule, he stopped practicing law and turned his sights to business endeavors where he earned even more success.

With the wealth he acquired from his companies, Follett hired Ammi Burnham Young to design a house for him and his family. There was no doubt that Young was a talented architect. He had already designed Vermont's second statehouse. But there was one part of the job that he and Timothy Follett argued about. Follett wanted a balcony on the front of his home, and Young refused, saying that the Greek Revival design he had chosen with the six impressive columns in front should not include a balcony. Eventually, Follett *mostly* got his way. (He was the one paying for the house, after all.) Young built the balcony, but there was no visible door leading to it. Instead, one of the large windows on the second floor was made to swing outward like a door. This allowed the Follett family to enjoy their balcony without Young compromising too much of his architectural design.

Upon completion, the Follett House immediately became a landmark of style on Burlington's waterfront, as well as a social center for the town. Loraine Follett, Timothy's wife, loved entertaining and hosted many teas and dinner parties at their home.

For a while, the Folletts' success continued to grow. Seeing a future in the railroad industry, Timothy began building a railroad from Boston to Burlington. When a man named Charles Paine started his own railroad company, the two ended up in a contest to see who would finish their track first. Follett won. However, his victory was short-lived when his rival won the rights to build the Rouse Point Bridge over Lake Champlain. Losing this important crossing ended Follett's career in the railroad. He lost his job and his fortune, and his health began failing again. At the end of his life, Timothy Follett had lost everything, including the beautiful home he'd put so much effort into building. To make matters worse, the man who bought the house was the chief engineer of the railroad company that had put Follett out of business.

Over the next several decades, the Follett House had many tenants. It was used for everything from a Red Cross to a kindergarten to a shelter for French war brides to an office for Catholic charities. It's not surprising, then, that these days it also houses a few ghosts.

The beautiful building at 63 College Street is currently the home of a real estate office, and some of the people who've worked there say it's definitely haunted. The clock in the owner's office seems to run on a different time than the rest of the world, lights tend to turn themselves back on after employees have left the building, and some unseen prankster likes to play jokes with the coffee maker.

The owner's assistant arrived early one morning to get work done before anyone else arrived. But first, of course, she made coffee. She put a clean filter in the machine, filled it with coffee, poured the water, and flipped the switch. But when she came back a few minutes later to fill her cup, the coffee pot was filled with dingy water, not coffee. The woman was confused because she knew she'd scooped the coffee into the filter. That's when something caught her attention: there in the trashcan was the filter full of coffee. Someone or something had thrown it away! Now, that's just wrong. Ghosts should never deprive a person of their caffeine. The woman left. She decided her work could wait until she was no longer alone in the office.

One of the spirits haunting the Follett House may have been that of Loraine Follett herself. An old portrait of Mrs. Follett used to frequently fall off the wall, and people reported feeling her presence in the building. Dr. Patrick McManaway, a practitioner of psychic and healing arts, visited the Follett House to help Loraine's restless spirit move on. Because of the ghost's strong attachment to her former home, she needed help leaving. Dr. McManaway sent a message to the other side, asking for someone to come guide her. Rather than a relative or single friendly spirit answering his call, a whole group of "party-goers" appeared, perhaps some of the guests who used to attend Mrs. Follett's many social gatherings. Dr. McManaway said the spirits "swooped in in droves and carried her away like a flock of birds." It was a very moving experience for him.

Loraine's spirit may be at peace now, but the Follett House still stands in Burlington, and it's still got a few interesting characters within its walls. Visitors better be nice to the ghosts there if they want a cup of coffee.

CHAPTER 7

The Hermit of Champlain and Other Harbor Haunts

Perhaps the most peculiar person who ever called Burlington home was Isaac Nye.

Isaac owned a piece of waterfront property on Battery Street where he built a small store with space for him to live in back. There he started managing the transporting of cargo boats on Lake Champlain. Nye was a hard worker who spent a lot of time making sure his business made a profit. But when he wasn't working, he engaged in a strange hobby: he attended funerals.

Isaac Nye never missed a chance to travel to the cemetery to join the mourners in laying a fellow citizen to rest, whether he knew the deceased or not. The image of him riding in his wagon at the back of a funeral procession became a well-known sight in Burlington.

Over the years, Isaac's odd behaviors increased. He spent more and more time alone, seemed to have no friends, and never spoke to anyone unless they spoke to him first. His unusual personality earned him the nickname "the Hermit of Champlain." He also began to make poor business decisions. He refused to sell some wooden masts for a good price, allowing them to rot instead. One day, he closed his store with no notice and didn't reopen it. No one knew why.

However, the store did open its doors one more time . . . in 1871, when Isaac Nye died. Isaac's last request was for his body to be laid out on the counter at his store so that people could visit and pay their respects. Picture the scene: a store that's been abandoned for years, dusty and covered with spiderwebs, with a corpse resting on the counter. Would you venture inside? Many people did. Their curiosity drove them. They wanted to get a glimpse of the Hermit of Champlain one more time.

Today, the location of Isaac Nye's store is the home of Burlington's beloved seafood restaurant Shanty on the Shore. Here, you can order delicious lobster and shrimp, but you might get a serving of spooky sensations on the side. Doors at Shanty on the Shore can be hard to open even when they're unlocked, and staff at the restaurant claim to feel the company of unseen spirits on their shifts. A manager alone in the building one night felt the presence of someone pass him on the stairs, and a waitress who worked at the Shanty in the 1990s sometimes had the sensation of being pushed by invisible hands when she was delivering food to customers.

The invisible specter who haunts the restaurant doesn't always stay invisible. One couple who dined there late one evening saw an elderly man dressed in all black standing outside staring up at the sky. When they walked closer to him, he disappeared.

These occurrences seem odd until you remember that the restaurant was the temporary resting place for Isaac Nye's body. It's no wonder that a building that once doubled as a funeral home has a ghost. Maybe the Hermit of Champlain is still there, wishing he had the place to himself again.

The spirit at Shanty on the Shore isn't the only ghost that haunts Burlington's waterfront. The *Phoenix* was a wooden steamship built in 1815. The historic boat was famous in Vermont and once carried President James Monroe across Lake Champlain. But the *Phoenix* met a tragic end on the night of September 4, 1819.

The ship's captain, Jahaziel Sherman, was sick with the flu the night the boat was scheduled to sail from Burlington to St. Johns, Quebec, so he asked his son Richard to command the voyage instead. The twenty-one-year-old took his job seriously, determined to make his father proud.

The *Phoenix* left Burlington at 11:00 P.M. under a full moon. It hadn't been on the water long when a fire broke out in the pantry of the ship. The strong night winds caused the fire to spread quickly until it was too large to control.

Richard Sherman did his best to save his passengers and crew. He fired a shot into the air to quiet the panic and gave orders to ready the lifeboats. The first lifeboat quickly filled and was successfully launched, saving the lives of more than twenty people. The second boat, however, encountered a problem. It had to be cut free before it was full, leaving eleven people stranded on the burning ship, including the young captain. Still determined to be a good leader, he told the others to try to cling to anything they could to stay afloat in the water. Richard followed his own advice and clung to a piece of a wooden table. The following morning, he was

found unconscious but alive. Six of the souls on board the *Phoenix*, however, did not survive.

No one knows whether the fire on the *Phoenix* was accidental or an act of foul play, but the sight of the flaming ship wasn't soon forgotten by the people who watched helplessly as it sank off the coast of Colchester Point. Even

two hundred years after the disaster, locals are still reminded of the fire on the *Phoenix*. Some say, on full moon nights, you can still see it burning out on the lake, its ghostly flames eerily illuminating the darkness.

CHAPTER 8

Memories Remain

People expect old places to be haunted. The longer a house or building has existed, and the more cobwebs found in its corners, the more people assume it has spooky stories to tell. But when it comes to hauntings, the age of a place is not the only factor to consider. New buildings can be haunted, too. So can people. Before you dismiss a place as "too young" to house a spirit, ask yourself where it was built and what lived (or died) on the land before. The answers may surprise you.

The South Meadow condominiums on Raymond Place were built in the 1980s, but some of the spirits that inhabit the units alongside the current residents go back much further than that. And there are a *lot* of spirits there.

One resident of the complex wasn't too surprised to experience supernatural phenomena. She comes from a long line of women with a gift for being able to see and hear things others can't. But even without her sensitivity to spirit energy, she wouldn't have been able to ignore some of the things that occurred in her apartment. When she first moved in, she unpacked a box of kitchen items and placed a stack of four wooden salad bowls in the cabinet. When she turned around, the stack of bowls came tumbling out as if knocked by an unseen hand. Unperturbed, she put them back again.

Strange encounters happened outside of the apartment too. While watching her daughter play on the playground, the woman felt the touch of a small hand on her hip. She turned, expecting to see a child trying to get her attention, but no one was there.

The woman's daughter must have inherited the family gift as well because a few weeks after they had moved into South Meadows, the little girl asked her mom to help with something. Her mother was busy in the kitchen at the time, so she asked her daughter to bring whatever it was in there. The three-year-old stopped in the doorway with a scared expression. "I can't," she said. "The lady doesn't want me to come in the kitchen." When the mother asked the little girl who she was talking about, she pointed to an empty spot in the room and described a woman in a white dress with long hair.

This South Meadow resident was not only a mother, she was also a middle school teacher, and she was not about to let her little girl be bullied by a ghost. She looked where her daughter had pointed and said, "*Everyone* is allowed in the kitchen." After that, there were no more problems in the kitchen, but the woman did sometimes see a shadowy shape hovering near the doorway.

Having stopped the ghostly bullying and set things in order, the resident thought her spiritual encounters were over.

Then a new sensation began to trouble her. She started waking up between eleven o'clock and midnight to the smell of something burning, but a source of the odor could never be found.

This apartment wasn't the only one haunted by a burning smell. A woman who lives with her husband in another part of the complex also wakes up at night to the smell of smoke. For her, the experience is particularly alarming because her own home burned down when she was young, so the scent of smoke brings back troubling memories. However, she isn't alone during these situations. The burning smell is always accompanied by a woman with long gray hair wearing a long white dress. She comforts the resident and tries to make her feel better.

Other people who live at South Meadow have also experienced strange phenomena. Some see shapes floating around or have trouble with electrical appliances turning on and off by themselves or just feel uncomfortable in certain places in their home. One woman's cat used to spend long stretches of time staring at one spot on the ceiling for no obvious reason.

Why does this 80s era condominium complex house so many restless spirits? The answers may be found by digging into the past.

During the Civil War, a marine hospital for treating wounded soldiers sat on the land beneath the South Meadow apartments, and in 1866 the grounds were sold for the creation of Burlington's Home for Destitute Children. Home Street, less than 300 feet from South Meadow's address, was named for this place. The purpose of the institution was to supply needy children with necessities and help educate them and teach them morals. However, some documents from the facility refer to the children as "inmates" and describe the process of hiring the children out for work. One document even mentioned that parents who sent their children to the home could later get them back "if the board chooses to return them." These details suggest that, while the foundation's mission seemed good-hearted, some of their methods may have been harsh.

Already, the existence of a Civil War hospital and a Home for Destitute Children on the grounds of the South Meadow condominiums help explain why ghosts have been sighted there. But an article in a Burlington newspaper from 1893 solidifies the connection.

On May 2, 1893, a fire broke out at the Home for Destitute Children. At the time, the building housed seventy-one children ages three months to eighteen years, in addition to the adults who attended them. Thankfully, everyone made it out alive, but it was a terrifying experience for everyone. The children, who had been sleeping when the fire started, were grabbed from their beds, many screaming as they were carried to safety.

A small hand reaching for an adult at a playground. A woman trying to keep a child out of a kitchen. A woman offering comfort during the night. The smell of smoke occurring at the same time every evening.

The South Meadow apartments may have only existed since the 1980s, but the memories of the land's previous inhabitants remain.

CHAPTER 9

Unexpected Encounters in South Burlington

There are certain moments in life that you always remember. Thea Lewis, Vermont native and host of Burlington's ghost tours, will never forget the first time she saw a ghost.

Just outside the charming Queen City Park neighborhood in South Burlington on the shore of Lake Champlain is a 100-acre nature area called Red Rocks Park. The park's scenic views, hiking trails, and swimming areas make it a popular recreation spot for locals and tourists alike. It was here, on an early morning walk, that Thea and her dog Zeus saw a ghost.

Zeus was a 105-pound, extremely friendly Rottweiler with a lot of energy. Just after six o'clock on a morning in autumn, he and his owner had the wildflower-strewn trails of Red Rocks Park pretty much to themselves. With the trees making a canopy above the path, it was still mostly dark, and Thea was walking slowly and using a flashlight to keep herself from tripping on tree roots, while her dog bounded ahead fearlessly. At only two years old, Zeus's obedience training was still in progress, and his enthusiasm sometimes got the best of him, so when he wagged his tail in excitement and sped up, Thea knew he had seen someone or something interesting.

Looking ahead, she saw a man standing on the trail. He hadn't been there a moment before. He wore a wool jacket and cap, like a Civil War soldier, but Thea wasn't thrown by his odd choice of clothing. Vermont locals often made unique style choices. She assumed he'd bought his outfit at a vintage clothing store. Seeing that her giant rottweiler was barreling toward the man, she shouted, "Don't worry! He's friendly!" But Ms. Lewis needn't worry about Zeus bowling the fellow over with his friendliness because at that moment, the man disappeared.

Both Thea and her dog stopped in their tracks, bewildered. Zeus looked back at his owner as if she could explain where the man went, but she was as startled as he was. She listened for the sound of footsteps in the woods. She walked to the spot where the man had been and peered into the trees and scanned the path ahead. There was no sign of him. Thea and her dog had just seen a ghost.

Although she wasn't particularly *afraid*, the encounter had unnerved Thea. She picked up her pace and steered her dog back to the main path that led home.

When Thea asked around about the apparition on the trail, she learned that she and Zeus were not the first to see him. Several other people had similar experiences. A man from New York, lost on his drive to Queen City Park, had pulled over by the entrance of Red Rock Park to ask directions of a man in uniform, but the man disappeared before he could speak to him. A young woman training for a marathon in the park saw the ghost standing near a horse in a pasture across the road. And a driver once caught a glimpse of a soldier in his rearview mirror as he drove by

the area. When he turned to get a better look, the image vanished.

Although no one knows who the ghost is, his clothing suggests he was a Civil War soldier, which makes sense when you know a bit more about the area. The Baxter Hospital, where Vermont's soldiers were treated during the war, used to reside on the land that borders, possibly even overlaps, where the park is today.

But the sighting of a lonely ghost soldier isn't the only eerie thing connected with Queen City Park. Originally owned by the Central Vermont Railroad, the area was a popular picnic spot for some of the country's most well-known families. However, by the late 1800s, Queen City Park had become a favorite meeting place for Spiritualists.

Followers of Spiritualism believe that the spirits of the dead can communicate with the living, and the practice was most widespread in America in the late 1800s and early 1900s. People known as mediums held séances to help the living contact their dead relatives. While some of these Spiritualists were the real thing and had the gift of intuition that enabled them to communicate with the deceased, many were con artists and frauds, scamming grief-stricken people out of their money and taking advantage of their emotions.

Harry Houdini, the famous magician, detested Spiritualists. After his mother died, he sought the help of a medium to contact her, but when he realized most were fake, he became enraged. Houdini began attending séances in disguise. In the middle of the act, he would leap up and shout, "I am Houdini! And YOU are a fraud!"

Two mediums famous nationwide for their ability to deliver messages to the living from their deceased loved ones were Maud

Lord-Drake and Nettie Clark, and both spent time in Queen City Park.

Mrs. Lord-Drake spent many nights holding candlelit séances in parlors or outside beneath the stars, helping Burlington residents communicate with friends and family on the other side. Her customers were frequently shocked at her ability to describe the dearly departed down to the tiniest detail. One night, she even connected with a spirit before his friends even knew he had died.

Maud had a group of people gathered around her table in Queen City Park when a spirit made himself known to her. She described the man, and he was immediately identified by a couple in the room. However, they told her she must be mistaken, for the man was still alive. In fact, they had just seen him in a town called Malone. The medium told the couple she was sorry, but their friend had indeed passed, and they would learn the truth soon. Before the end of the night, a telegram arrived from Malone confirming the news. Their friend had died.

Nettie Clark, another famous medium, held séances in the hotel she ran in Queen City Park in the 1920s and then later in her home on North Street in Burlington. Attendees reported floating tables and flying objects during Nettie's sessions, as well as her uncanny ability to share things about the deceased that no stranger could possibly know.

Perhaps all those séances in the early 1900s can explain some of the unexpected visitors at Queen City Park in recent years. Witnesses have reported ghostly forms on the beach after dark, as well as the spirits of two ladies dressed up in large-brimmed hats walking arm in arm near the location of the old hotel. One resident of the current neighborhood even woke at three o'clock in the morning to find a man in a suit sitting on his front porch smoking a pipe. The man belonged to a long-gone era.

It's no wonder that ghosts flock to this area. After so many years of mediums drawing spirits to South Burlington, they probably feel welcome there. Some of them may still have messages they need to share with the living. So, keep your eyes and ears open if you visit Red Rocks Park. Maybe one of the ghosts will choose to communicate with *you*.

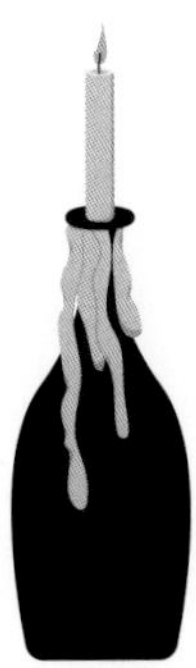

Winooski Lake

CHAPTER 10

Winooski's Wandering Spirits

Just outside of Burlington is a town that refuses to be outdone by the ghosts of the Queen City. Winooski houses a few haunts of their own, and the stories of these specters will send shivers up your spine.

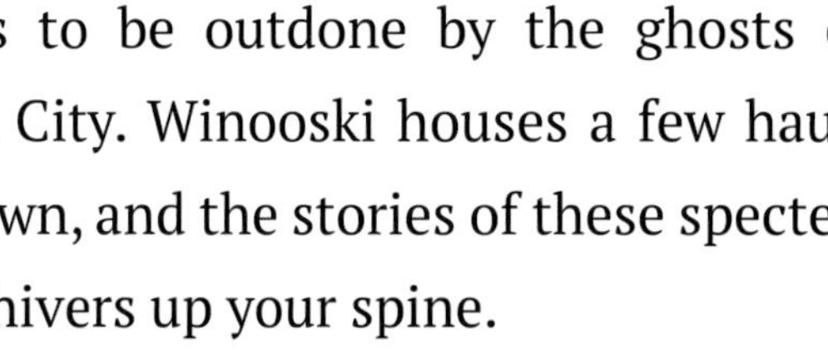

The White Horse of Winooski Valley Park

Some residents of Winooski have seen something that made their hearts gallop. Hikers and sightseers at Winooski Valley Park expect to encounter birds and beavers and other local wildlife, but some have been shocked to see a white horse running through the park. The animal is gorgeous, but ghostly. Witnesses say the horse prances through the grass, its beautiful mane flowing behind it. But if they get too close, the horse vanishes right before their eyes.

Why would the ghost of a white horse be haunting Winooski? There's a theory that this otherworldly creature might be the spirit of Revolutionary War hero Ethan Allen.

In the late 1700s, Ethan Allen fought for Vermont's statehood, and he used to live on the land that is now Winooski Valley Park. Allen believed in reincarnation, the idea that after death, a soul returns to earth in a new body. More than once, he claimed that when he died, he would come back as a white stallion.

Is one of Vermont's founders haunting Winooski Valley Park in the form of a horse? We can't know for sure, and so far, the white stallion hasn't stuck around long enough to answer questions.

A Haunted Bridge

The Blue Bridge over the Winooski River is not made for pedestrians, but that doesn't stop people from using the railroad bridge as a shortcut between Burlington and Winooski. Not only is this path illegal, it's also dangerous. Multiple deaths have occurred at the Blue Bridge over the years. Some of the victims died by suicide, others by accident. Regardless of the cause of death, it seems that at least one of the deceased souls has decided to stick around.

Several trespassers on the Blue Bridge have reported seeing a figure walking toward them down the tracks, but as the distance between them grows narrower, the mysterious figure disappears.

One man believes the spirit that haunts the bridge is a friendly ghost. On April 11, 2002, Paul Wilk went to Burlington after work to meet some friends for drinks. Afterward, he chose to walk home via the Blue Bridge. On the way across, Wilk realized he'd dropped his wallet. He got down on his hands and knees on the bridge to search for it, using a lighter to see by. Tired from work and possibly a little intoxicated, Wilk slipped and fell off the bridge.

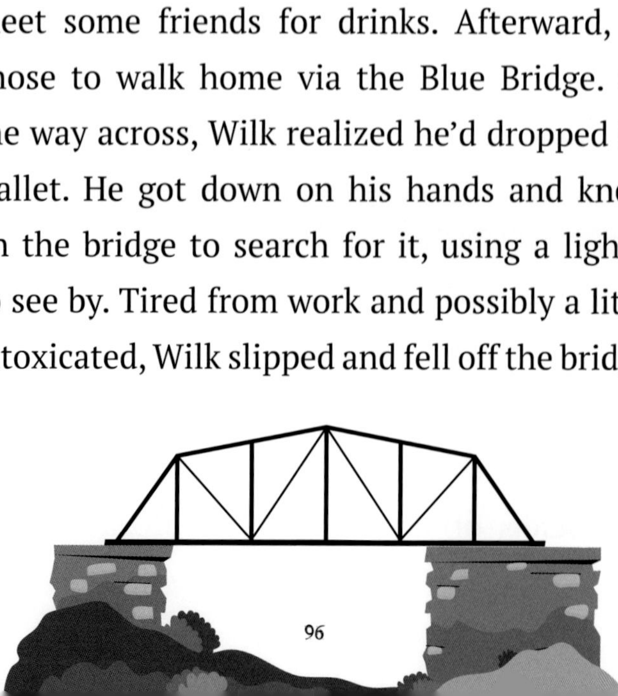

On the way down, the terrified man prayed to hit something soft.

Paul Wilk landed in the mud near the river and was knocked unconscious. When he awoke, he had a collapsed lung and several broken ribs. Still, he'd been lucky. A large log lay on one side of him, a rock on the other. His head had missed a boulder by only a few feet. Despite his injuries, he crawled a quarter of a mile to a water treatment plant. The following morning, someone found him and got help.

But Wilk thinks there was more than luck at play that night. He believes the spirit of the Blue Bridge saved him. He even got his wallet back. A week after his accident, someone found it and returned it to him.

School Spirits

Students and staff at Winooski High claim the school is haunted. When you find out what the gym was used for one day over sixty years ago, you'll understand why.

In August of 1960, a terrible car crash in Vermont took the lives of seven young men ages eighteen to twenty. The boys were all recent graduates of Winooski High School, and they had been out having a night of fun that may have included underage drinking. On the way home, they were driving way too fast on a slippery road when they lost control of their

car and crashed into a large maple tree. No one survived.

This terrible tragedy rocked the town of Winooski. Everyone knew one or more of the deceased boys or their families, and the collective grief overwhelmed the small town. So many people wanted to pay their respects to the dead that no funeral home was large enough to handle the huge crowd. Instead, two of the boys were taken to a funeral home while the memorial for the other five occurred at the high school.

On a Wednesday morning in August 1960, five caskets sat side by side in the Winooski High gymnasium. The parking lot overflowed with cars, and hundreds of mourners filed into a space normally used for basketball games and dances to say goodbye to five young lives cut short.

Not long after the funeral, reports of hauntings began. Objects have been known to lift themselves into the air without the help of humans, and a man performing in a play in the gym got an unpleasant shock when a piece of athletic equipment randomly fell off the wall onto his head as he stood backstage. But most of the stories related to Winooski High School involve eerie sounds.

Witnesses describe disembodied male voices calling to each other in the empty halls and the sounds of multiple lockers slamming at once even when no one is around. People alone in the gym after hours have heard the sound of feet running up and down the bleachers and sneakers squeaking on the gym floor. But the most unsettling noise heard at Winooski High is the sound of wheels rolling down the hall, perhaps the wheels of five caskets making their way to the gym.

The Ghost Girl

Winooski locals who aren't interested in ghosts can choose to stay away from these schools, parks, and bridges, but residents of the Woolen Mill Apartments can't escape spirits even in their own home.

Thea Lewis doesn't shy away from ghosts. In fact, she spends her evenings giving tours of haunted places in and around Burlington. Lewis is used to spooky stories and often meets people with their own tales about otherworldly encounters, but once in a while she hears a story that makes even her heart skip a beat.

One night just before Halloween, a man stuck around after Lewis's ghost tour to ask her advice. He wanted to know how to get rid of a ghost.

The man lived in the Woolen Mill Apartments, which had once been the site of an actual sawmill. In the 1800s, before child labor laws were passed, orphans and children of poor families were forced into hard labor. Instead of going to school, they worked long hours in mills and factories for very little money. This man told the tour guide that he was visited every night by the ghost of a little girl dressed like a factory worker. The first time he saw her standing in the corner of his bedroom, he closed his eyes and opened them again, hoping the image would be gone. It wasn't.

The ghost girl said, "Help me." In a soft voice, she told the terrified man she couldn't find her parents and asked him to come with her.

Can you imagine waking up in your bedroom and seeing the spirit of a frightened little girl begging you for help?

Thea Lewis gently asked the man if he had tried to talk to the ghost. She suggested he tell the girl he was not the right person to help her and ask her to leave. The man shook his head.

He said he was afraid to approach the ghost because of the "dark people." Apparently, when the little girl visited his bedroom at night, she wasn't alone. A crowd of people made of darkness and noise came with her. They don't talk, he told the tour guide, they just watch.

The man couldn't afford to move, but he was so unnerved by the nightly experiences that he went to a doctor for a medication to help him sleep, in hopes that he would not be

awakened by the little girl's pleas. Now, he was seeking advice from the tour guide.

Lewis felt sorry for the man, who was obviously distraught. Before they parted, she again encouraged him to try to communicate with the ghost girl. Whether he ever did is unknown. Maybe instead, he got enough money to move. Maybe the little girl and her friends are still there waiting for a new tenant to haunt.

CHAPTER 11

A Final Farewell

Life is full of mysteries, and death is full of even more. It's impossible to know what waits for us on the other side, why some ghosts remain attached to the living, or why some locations seem to encourage the deceased to stick around. But based on the number of supernatural sightings in the Queen City, one thing is certain: the spirits of Burlington's past are in good company.

Carie Juettner was born on Halloween and has loved ghost stories ever since. By day, she is a middle school English teacher, but by night, she is a writer of poems and short stories and novels. Carie lives in Austin, Texas, with her husband and pets, but she loves to travel. One of her favorite things to do on vacation is visit cemeteries and learn about local lore.

Check out some of the other Spooky America titles available now!

Spooky America was adapted from the creeptastic Haunted America series for adults. Haunted America explores historical haunts in cities and regions across America. Each book chronicles both the widely known and less-familiar history behind local ghosts and other unexplained mysteries. Here's more from *Haunted Burlington: Spirits of Vermont's Queen City* author, Thea Lewis: